WHOOPI GOLDBERG

Sugar Plum Ballerinas

Terrible Terrel

Sugar Plum Ballerinas

WHOOPI GOLDBERG
Sugar Plum Ballerinas
Terrible Terrel

with Deborah Underwood
Illustrated by Maryn Roos

DISNEP JUMP AT THE SUN BOOKS
New York

For Ma, who always dances . . .

Text copyright © 2010 by Whoopi Goldberg
Illustrations © 2010 by Maryn Roos

First Edition
1 3 5 7 9 10 8 6 4 2
V567-9638-5-10196

Printed in the United States of America

This book is set in 13 pt. Baskerville BT.
Reinforced binding

Library of Congress Cataloging-in-Publication Data on file.
ISBN 978-1-4231-2082-7 (hardcover)
ISBN 978-0-7868-5263-5 (paperback)

Visit sugarplumballerinas.com,
www.jumpatthesun.com, and
www.hyperionbooksforchildren.com

SUSTAINABLE FORESTRY INITIATIVE

Certified Fiber
Sourcing

www.sfiprogram.org

THIS LABEL APPLIES TO TEXT STOCK

Chapter 1

I stand in our kitchen, surveying a mass of grocery bags with satisfaction. Shopping mission accomplished in record time, thanks to me, Commander Terrel.

Dad puts the last bag on the counter. "You sure you got this, sweetheart?" he asks me.

I nod. "Edward can help," I say.

My brother Edward, who is leaning against the counter messing with his phone, looks up but doesn't object. Danny, Cheng, and Tai fled to their rooms the second we got back from the store. Danny, who's twenty-two, said that after all that shopping, he couldn't stand to look at food ever again, but I notice he took an entire package of cookies into his room with him.

"Okay," Dad says. "I'm going to get a haircut."

"Now?" I ask. Who gets a haircut at seven o'clock at night?

"Last appointment of the day," Dad says. "Take care of your sister, Edward."

I roll my eyes. Like I need Edward to take care of me. I am the taking-care-of-things person in this house, and everyone knows it. Besides, Edward is only twelve. That's just three-and-a-quarter-years older than me.

Dad kisses me on the top of the head and leaves.

Time to get to work.

"Atten-*tion*," I say.

Edward shakes his head at me. "Do you *have* to do that 'attention' thing?"

"Apparently, I do," I say, staring at his thumbs, which are still jumping around the keyboard of his phone.

He sighs, puts the phone away, and salutes.

"Yes, ma'am. Where do we start?"

I smile. That's more like it.

You might wonder why this older brother actually listens to me. Actually, all of my older brothers listen to me. Why? Because they know what's good for them.

Our mom died when I was only six. So, I am in charge of keeping the house running smoothly. Nobody makes me; I do it because I like it and I'm good at it. Some people are good at spelling, or at running. I, personally, am an organizing genius (if I do say so myself). My friends come to me when they need help, because I can think through problems and find answers. Even when I was little, I could see what needed to be done, and then *get* it done.

I assign each of my brothers (except the oldest one, Waylon—he has his own apartment now) a cleaning job every week. When we go shopping, I call the shots, sending them each out on cereal or banana missions while my dad and I pack things neatly into the shopping cart. I keep a big yellow binder full of vital information, such as when Edward needs to get his field-trip permission slip back to school, when my dad needs to write the rent check, when Tai needs to have his science project done, and how much toilet paper we have left.

At first, my brothers and my dad were not happy about having a little kid boss them around. Since they didn't understand why they should let me run everything, I went on strike. I hid the binder under my bed, sat back, and watched everything fall apart.

Which it did.

"We're out of soy milk," Tai hollered at breakfast one day.

"Yep," I said.

"Is it the thirty-first already?" Dad said, pushing his glasses up on his nose as he stared at the calendar. "Our rent is almost late!"

"Yep," I said.

"I can't find my homework!" Edward yelled from the living room. "There are stupid papers all over the floor!"

"Yep," I said.

"No toilet paper!" Danny howled from the bathroom.

"Interesting," I said, flipping the pages of my puzzle magazine.

Needless to say, in three days they had surrendered and promised to listen to me in the future.

So, now everything runs smoothly. No problems. No surprises. I love it. Dad is always saying that they'd never survive without me. This makes me feel good. It's also true.

Edward leans over and starts taking things out of a shopping bag. He holds up a jar of peanut butter. "Third cupboard, right?"

"Second cupboard, lower shelf," I say correcting him. The lower-shelf part is important.

Although my organizing ability is enormous, I am quite small. Any food that I might need to get by myself has to go on a lower shelf, and peanut butter is definitely something I need. "But do the frozen food first."

I put the spaghetti in the middle drawer, where it belongs. Although I like putting groceries away, it's not as much fun as usual. Something's bugging me. It takes a minute for me to figure out what it is.

"Hey, Edward. Why do you think Dad's

getting his hair cut so late?"

Edward takes out a handful of crackers and starts eating them as he puts the box away. "I dunno, T.," he says. "Who cares when he gets his hair cut?"

I care, because I know for a fact that Dad usually gets his hair cut every six weeks on a Saturday afternoon while I'm at ballet.

"Maybe the barber is going on vacation," Edward says.

Oh. I hadn't thought of that. "Yeah, probably," I say.

With both of us putting things away, unloading the groceries goes fast. When we're done, I make myself a bowl of Applesauce Surprise—my own special concoction that's made with applesauce, raisins, cinnamon, and gummy worms all mixed up together. I sit at the kitchen table, chomp down on a gummy worm—and start doing my homework.

Dad comes home with pizza for dinner.

But he also has a shopping bag stuffed under his coat as if he's trying to hide it.

"What's that?" I ask.

"Nothing," he says. "I just picked up a few new shirts on the way home."

Okay. Now that's *really* weird. Dad hates shopping for clothes. I don't remember him ever buying new clothes, except when Uncle Charlie got married and Dad had to buy black socks to wear with his rented tuxedo.

After I'm supposed to be in bed, I walk by Dad's room. He's standing in front of his mirror. He smiles, then stops, then smiles again. It looks like he's practicing his smile. I stand in the shadows and watch him do this for about five whole minutes.

I hope he's not losing his mind, I think as I walk back to bed. Organizing four boys and a dad is hard enough without the dad being crazy.

Chapter 2

Epatha and I sit outside on the steps of the Nutcracker School of Ballet even though it's late November and it's freezing. A gust of wind makes the dried brown leaves scuttle across the ground. Epatha's hair flies out in all directions. I pull my coat tighter around me. I almost mention Dad smiling in the mirror the other night to Epatha. But he didn't do anything weird today. Maybe he just had something stuck in his teeth.

Epatha interrupts my thoughts. "Have you seen those posters for *Sleeping Beauty*?" she asks. "It looks fabulous. *Fantastico. Fabuloso.*"

As usual, Epatha is speaking in English, Italian, and Spanish all at once (she lives with not only her mom, dad, and older sisters, but also her Puerto Rican grandma and her Italian grandma).

"Yeah, I've seen them. *Everyone's* seen them," I say. The posters are plastered all over the place.

Epatha pulls out a roll of strawberry-flavored hard candy and offers me a piece. As I pop it into my mouth, she squints thoughtfully. "I would totally love to go. But I'll bet it costs a billion trillion bucks a ticket."

I nod. I kind of wish she hadn't brought it up. It would be amazing to go, but I'm sure we can't afford it. I know exactly how much we spend on groceries each week. And if we spend that much on groceries, I'm sure we don't have a spare billion trillion bucks.

JoAnn thumps up the street toward us. Her leg has been in a lime green cast since she tripped on her skateboard last week, but she moves even faster with crutches than she did without them. The other two triplets, Jessica and Jerzey Mae, struggle to keep up with her.

"What are you crazy girls doing out here in the cold?" JoAnn asks. The crutches must be making her arms even stronger, because somehow she hauls me up into a standing position. I allow myself to be dragged up the remaining stairs and into the school. The others follow.

Even though JoAnn won't be able to dance for a while, she comes to class to see us. When we're dancing, she sits on the side of the room and reads. Usually.

"*Please* tell me she brought a book today," I mutter to Jessica.

Last ballet class, JoAnn forgot her book, so she spent the whole class watching us like a hawk, then whispering hints to each of us about what we were doing wrong. "Your arm's supposed to be higher, T.," she

11

told me. "Hey, Brenda—watch your back leg on those jumps," she hissed. By the end of class, we all wanted to clobber her, broken leg or not.

"She has at least two," Jessica says. "Jerzey and I each brought one in case she forgot." JoAnn even got on Jessica's nerves last time, and that's not easy to do.

Epatha looks around the room as if she's lost something. "Hey, where's Mason?" she asks.

"You mean Mr. Ballet?" JoAnn asks. Mason, the triplets' little brother, has been coming to our class for a while. It turns out he's some kind of ballet prodigy, picking up all the moves without even having to think about it. He even saved the triplets' dance at our recital by taking JoAnn's place after she wrecked her leg.

"He got so ballet crazy after that recital that Mom signed him up for a boys' ballet class,"

Jessica says as we enter the school's waiting room. "She found one that's not far from here and meets at the same time as ours."

I'm suddenly aware of someone glaring at me. "Hi, Midget," says that stuck-up-looking kid wearing a pink tiara. Tiara Girl hates all of us for no reason. Okay, fine—she was so obnoxious to us from the start that I started doing stuff like tying knots in her sneaker laces when she wasn't looking; so maybe now she has a *little* bit of a reason.

She's especially snotty to me. I think it's because I'm younger and shorter than the other girls in the class. Brenda thinks it's because I'm better at ballet than Tiara Girl is and she's jealous. It doesn't matter. It's like having an annoying fly in the room with you for a few hours a week—no big deal. Although I admit sometimes I wish I had a flyswatter.

"Back off, Tiara Noggin," Epatha says before I can open my mouth. It's nice to have someone stick up for me, although I'm quite capable of taking care of myself (I do have a bunch of older brothers, after all). It saves me the trouble of having to hide a rotten banana in Tiara Girl's dance bag.

We sit on the benches and start to dig around in our bags for our ballet slippers. Al and Brenda walk in together.

"Guys hi," Brenda says, talking backward as usual. "There out freezing it's."

Al's hat is a puffy silver cone that covers her from her head almost down to her eyeballs. "I know, I know," she says, peeling it off. "It's part of a new outfit Mom's making. She says it's a statement about the consumer society vacuuming out everyone's brains. But it also happens to be extremely warm, and I lost my other hat at the ice rink."

Al's mom is a fashion designer. We're used to seeing Al's mom in dramatic outfits, but Al doesn't usually wear silver cones on her head; she mostly dresses like a normal kid.

Ms. Debbé, our teacher, appears in the doorway. It must be weird-hat day, because she's wearing an orange and red fabric turban that's so tall I'm amazed she fits through the doorway. A long skirt made of the same material swirls around her ankles, and a big chunky orange necklace is draped around her neck.

"Wow," Epatha breathes. She is a big fan

of bright colors. "I totally want a turban like that."

"Right," says JoAnn. "I can just see you outside playing kickball at recess with that thing on your head."

Ms. Debbé thumps her walking stick on the floor for attention. "Ladies—the class, it begins!" She turns and heads up the stairs, and we follow.

Chapter 3

Before long, we've warmed up and done our barre exercises. Now we're leaping across the floor. My heart races as I bound across the room, stretching my legs out as far as I can.

I love ballet. It's a very organized art form. It's not like baseball, where you're never quite sure where the ball you hit will go. You do a plié, and it will be a plié, unless you screw it up, which I don't. You do a chassé, and it will be a chassé. We always start our classes at the barre, then do floor work. The order never changes. You always know what you're going to be doing.

The sky outside glows yellow. The smell of

crisp, fresh air drifts in through the window that's cracked open. Just a few more minutes of class left. My brother Cheng will be waiting for me outside, as always. My family is going grocery shopping tonight, which is one of my favorite things to do. I feel a little smile creep onto my face. Life is pretty darned good.

"Chaîné turns, ladies," Ms. Debbé calls. "Two at a time, if you please."

We all head over to the sides of the room and arrange ourselves in two bunches. My friends and I stand in one group, because we always do.

The music starts. "Ready? Go!" says Ms. Debbé.

We spin across the floor two at a time. Epatha goes first, along with a red-haired girl from the other group. Then Brenda goes, then Jerzey, then Jessica, then Al. Then it's my turn. I look at the other group to see who I'll be spinning with. Of course—Tiara Girl.

I don't mind. I'll show off my turns against hers any day. She glares at me. Frankly, if she acted like a human, *I* wouldn't know how to act. I glower back at her, because that's what I always do, and we start turning.

She's taller than me—just like everyone else, since I'm the youngest one in the class—and has longer legs. But I can spin faster. We're both trying to get to the other side of the room first. I can see her pulling ahead of me. No way. With a burst of energy, I spin, spin, spin until I reach the other side of the room just a fraction of a second ahead of her.

Tiara Girl tosses her head, as if to pretend she didn't just lose the chaîné turns Olympics. I ignore her, act like kicking her butt in a race is no big deal. But inside I'm jumping up and down and singing, *Nyah nyah nyah nyah nyaaaah!*

"It is not a race, ladies," Ms. Debbé says in her thick French accent. "Ballerinas, they are graceful, yes? They are not bomber planes running across the sky."

I picture a bomber with little legs galloping overhead and almost laugh out loud.

After the last girls spin their way across the floor, Ms. Debbé shuts off the music and claps her hands for attention. "Now," she says, "please sit for one moment."

We sit in clusters around Ms. Debbé, which gives us a good view of her feet. She's wearing orange and red sandals that are so bright they look radioactive.

Epatha can't contain herself. "Amazing shoes, Ms. Debbé," she says, staring at them as if she were mesmerized.

Ms. Debbé looks surprised. "Why, thank you, Miss Epatha." She smiles, then continues. "You may know that the Ballet Company of London will be performing in town for the next several weeks."

Lots of heads nod. As I said before, you'd

have to be dead not to have seen the posters.

"I encourage you to go if you can. There is nothing like live ballet to inspire your dancing. This ballet, the *Sleeping Beauty*, is a Very Important Ballet. And this performance, it will be glorious." Ms. Debbé sweeps her arm in a half circle for emphasis, her shawl fluttering.

Glorious. I've never seen a ballet—I mean, a *real* ballet, with sets and costumes and everything. Our school shows are fun to dance in, but I would not call them glorious. For the show last summer, most of us had to wear big fuzzy purple monster costumes. It is safe to say that we did not look even a little bit glorious. All of a sudden, seeing a glorious ballet seems like the most important thing in the world.

"Also," Ms. Debbé continues, "the holidays, they are almost upon us. And of course we will have our annual holiday party. It will be the Saturday before Christmas. If you think you know an adult who could help organize it, please do let me know after. . . ."

Epatha raises her hand. "My parents can probably make some food for it."

"Very good, Epatha. Thank you. Now . . ."

Across the room, Tiara Girl's hand shoots into the air.

"My aunt can organize the whole party," she says in a loud voice. "*She'll* make sure everything's done right," she adds. She gives Epatha one of her trademark snotty looks, as if to say Epatha's parents would screw things up for sure.

Epatha turns to face Tiara Girl and is about to open her mouth when Ms. Debbé says, "Very good, ladies. We will decide the details later."

Epatha looks as if she might explode. "Chill, E.," I say in a low voice. "She's a stupid twerp. Not worth getting upset over."

"Class dismissed," Ms. Debbé says quickly. I guess if Epatha and Tiara Girl are going to start socking each other, Ms. Debbé would rather they do it outside.

We all tromp downstairs and grab our stuff. "You guys want to come over after school tomorrow?" Epatha asks as we head outside. Her family owns a restaurant, Bella Italia.

"Sure," Brenda says, and we all agree.

Parents and other people waiting to pick up kids are standing around outside talking. I look around for Cheng, but I don't see him. That's weird—he's tall, so he's pretty hard to miss. And he never forgets to pick me up.

"Terrel! Over here."

I see my dad waving. As I walk over, he says something to the lady standing next to him.

"Hey, Dad. What are you doing here?" I ask. Dad picks me up on Saturdays, but not on Tuesdays.

He clears his throat. "Oh, I . . . I got off work early, so I told Cheng I'd pick you up. That okay?" he asks, smiling at me.

"'Course!" I say. I wave to my friends and start to walk away, but Dad doesn't follow me. "Are you coming?"

He says good-bye to the lady and takes a few quick steps to catch up with me. "How was class?" he asks.

"Fine," I say. "Same as always."

"And that's good, right?" he asks, raising an eyebrow.

"Yup," I say, grinning.

"Do you know a girl named April?" Dad asks as we turn on to our street.

"April?" I say, shifting my backpack to my other shoulder. "I don't think so."

Dad waves to our neighbor Mr. Slotnik, who is peering out the window, as always. "There's not an April in your ballet class?" he asks.

I think about all the people in ballet. There are a few new kids, and I don't know all their names yet. Maybe it's one of them.

Then I remember: Tiara Girl's name is April. We just call her Tiara Girl so much that I forget.

"Ewww!" I say. "Yes, I know an April. She's horrible. She's really snotty to us, and she wears this tiara all the time. *All* the time." We start up our apartment stairs. "Why?" I ask.

He looks a bit shocked by my reaction. "Uh, no reason," he says. "I was just talking to her aunt outside class and wondered if you knew her."

I snort. "I wish I didn't," I say, dropping my backpack onto the chair.

Dad takes off his coat and hangs it by the door. "Now, Terrel," he says, "that's not very nice. Maybe she's one of those people who seems aloof until you get to know her."

I'm not sure what *aloof* means, but I *am*

sure that getting to know Tiara Girl is never going to be on my to-do list. But Dad is very gentle, kind of like Jessica. He doesn't ever seem to get angry at anybody, even us kids when we do stupid things. So explaining to him exactly how annoying Tiara Girl is would be pointless.

"Yeah, maybe," I say, to get him off the subject.

Dad drops me off at home, then says he's going to run back to the office for a while.

"I thought you said you got off work early," I say.

"Did I? I meant that I just took a little time off so I could pick you up from class," he says.

This makes no sense at all. Why would Dad take time off from work just to pick me up?

Why do I get the feeling he's not telling me everything?

Chapter 4

On Friday, Dad gets home just as I finish my math homework. He hangs his coat by the door, but on the wrong hook. I've very carefully labeled all the hooks with our names so we can keep track of where our coats are, especially since my brothers' coats all look the same.

"*Dad*."

He looks at his watch. His eyes dart around the room.

"*Dad*," I say again.

He finally turns his head in my direction. "Yes, sweetheart?"

I point toward the door. "Wrong hook."

He stares uncomprehendingly. Finally he

sees what he's done and moves his coat.

"What are we having for dinner?" I ask. My stomach rumbles even though I had some Applesauce Surprise earlier; it's colorful, but not very filling.

I follow Dad into the kitchen. He's walking really fast for some reason. Once we're there, he pulls out a big pot and begins to fill it with water.

"I'm going to make spaghetti for you and your brothers. But I won't be eating with you. I have an appointment." Dad starts opening and closing cupboards—first the top left, then the top right, then the bottom left, then the bottom right.

"What are you looking for?" I say. "The spaghetti sauce is in the back of the top left cupboard. Spaghetti is in the middle drawer."

"Ah, yes," he says, lunging for the drawer.

He *knows* where the stuff is. He and I spent one afternoon last year working out exactly where everything should go, and it hasn't changed since then. I wonder if our real dad was kidnapped by a UFO. Maybe this is some weird alien dad sent to spy on us or eat our brains. Maybe Dad really *is* losing it.

The pot in the sink is overflowing. I run to turn off the tap. "*Another* appointment?" I ask. "What kind of appointment do you have at night?"

Dad grunts as he lifts the pot of water and carries it to the stove. "Nothing important," he says. "I'm just meeting someone." He turns on the burner, then rushes out of the kitchen, tripping on Danny's sneakers as he goes.

Fifteen minutes later, I'm mixing up the spaghetti and sauce on the stove. Edward is setting the table, and my other brothers are scattered all over the apartment. Dad has disappeared into his room, coming out only to help strain the spaghetti before disappearing again.

As I stir, I smell something weird. Kind of like a pine forest—an extremely stinky pine forest.

"How's it coming?" asks Dad, who is right behind me. I sniff. He must have gone swimming in a pool of aftershave. I can barely breathe.

I turn to face him. His newly cut hair is slicked to one side, and he's wearing a dark red sweater I've never seen before. He usually wears normal button-down shirts and jeans, but now he's wearing gray flannel pants. He looks like a kid whose mom has dressed him up for the school picture.

"Uh . . . good," I say, trying not to

gag. I go over to the garbage can and pretend to throw something out so I can get a gulp of non-pine-forest air.

Danny comes into the room, followed by Tai and Cheng. "Wow," he says. "Looking good, Dad!" He gives Dad a thumbs-up, grabs a plate of spaghetti, and takes it to his room.

Dad seems embarrassed but pleased. He glances at me, almost like he wants *me* to say he looks good, too. I give him a weak smile. I guess he looks okay, but he sure doesn't smell good. I like his normal smell, which is just soap.

"All right, kids," he says. "I'll be back by nine. I have my phone if you need me." He checks his watch again, then races out the front door.

"What the heck was that about?" I ask.

Cheng and Tai exchange a quick look. "Nothing, T.," Tai says. "He's just meeting someone, that's all." He loads spaghetti onto his plate and then puts some on a plate for me.

Then a horrible thought pops into my head. I'll bet Dad got fired.

If he was fired, that would explain why he could pick me up from ballet on Tuesday. He'd need the new clothes and haircut if he had to start looking for a new job. It would even explain his practicing his smiles in front of the mirror; everyone knows you have to make a good first impression. And he wouldn't have told us because he wouldn't have wanted us to be worried.

The more I think about it, the more this makes sense. And I *am* worried. What'll happen to us if Dad can't find another job? I slowly chew on strands of spaghetti. I wonder if I should say anything to my brothers. They probably haven't figured it out yet. But I decide not to—not till I'm sure.

Chapter 5

"*¿Qué pasa,* Terrel?" Epatha asks. "What is *up* with you?"

All the Sugar Plum Sisters—me, Epatha, Al, Brenda, Jerzey Mae, Jessica, and JoAnn— are sitting at our favorite booth in Bella Italia after ballet class on Saturday. We're chomping our way through a basket of garlic breadsticks. All of us except Jerzey are drinking Bella Bombshells, Epatha's invention. She makes them by mixing all the soda flavors together. Jerzey can't deal with Bombshells, which do look kind of like swamp water, so she's sipping lemon-lime soda delicately through a straw. Maybe I should have asked for that instead. My stomach feels a little funny, and I'm not sure pouring a Bombshell into it is a good idea.

It takes me a minute to realize that Epatha has been talking to me. "What?" I ask.

Epatha passes me a roll of candies—lime ones this time. I take one and suck on it without really tasting it.

"You haven't said a word all afternoon," she says, tossing her bright purple scarf around her neck dramatically.

Epatha's mom comes over. "More breadsticks, girls?"

"Yes, please," says Al, passing her the empty basket.

"Is something wrong, Terrel?" Jessica asks, her eyebrows wrinkled in concern.

I shake my head. "My dad's just acting weird, that's all," I say.

Epatha laughs. "*All* dads act weird," she says loudly so her dad will hear her. He's over by the restaurant entrance, whistling as he scrawls the evening specials on the board. He stops whistling, shakes his fist at Epatha, then winks.

"What do you mean, weird?" JoAnn asks.

"He's just kind of distracted," I say. I don't tell them about his hanging his coat on the wrong hook, because none of them except Jerzey Mae would understand how wrong that is.

I take a breath, then say quickly, to get it over with, "I'm afraid he might have lost his job."

"What?" says JoAnn.

"Oh, no," says Jessica, putting her hand on my arm.

I nod. "He had some appointment last night. I think it was a job interview. He got dressed up, and he stank like pine trees."

Epatha drops her breadstick melodramatically. "He was wearing *cologne*? Your dad?"

I shrug. "Yeah. So?"

Epatha raises her eyebrows knowingly. "He's going out at night, wearing cologne; *I* know what's going on," she says. She bends forward and talks more softly, so we all have to lean forward to hear her. "He's got himself a girlfriend."

"A *what*?" I yell. My friends back away. Jerzey Mae clutches her ears.

"A girlfriend," Epatha says again, in a matter-of-fact way.

I shake my head so fast it feels like my hair will fall off. "No, no, no. Dads do not have girlfriends."

JoAnn takes another breadstick from the basket. "Some of them do."

"*Mine* doesn't."

Jessica opens her mouth, closes it, then says hesitantly, "Terrel, it might be nice for your dad to have a girlfriend." Jessica is very romantic. She writes poetry and stuff. So I'm not surprised she'd say something insane like this.

"Yeah—it might be great," Al says.

What? I'd expect Al to have better sense. She just about had a heart attack when her mom went out on a date with the UPS delivery guy. "No, it would *not* be nice," I say. "And it would *not* be great. It would be ridiculous. *Ri-dic-u-lous*," I say, shredding my breadstick into teensy pieces.

"But don't you want him to get married again someday?" Jessica blurts out.

I nearly choke on the lime candy that's still in my mouth.

"I mean, don't you get tired of being the only girl in your family?" Jessica adds.

Jerzey Mae nods, her pink-ribboned pony-tails bobbing up and down. "And you could be in the wedding and wear a pink dress. And she would do some of the house things, so you wouldn't have to help your dad so much. Like the grocery shopping—"

"You know I *like* doing the grocery

shopping!" I say. I'm annoyed that my friends don't get how serious this is. My family doesn't need anyone coming around and changing things. We're fine just the way we are. After my mom died, we had all the change we could handle. I'll be happy if nothing except my underwear changes for the rest of my life.

I lower my voice a little. "And, no, it

would *not* be nice for me to have another girl around," I say. "I can run everything perfectly fine by myself." I slam my cup down on the table.

"Holy cow. Calm down, T.," Epatha says. "You're turning purple."

"Deep breaths, Terrel," Brenda says. She wants to be a doctor when she grows up. I guess she knows enough not to talk backward during a possible medical emergency. "Easy. In. Out."

I breathe in and out slowly a few times. "He does not have a girlfriend. End of discussion."

The other girls look at each other. "Fine," says Epatha. "But keep your eye out for signs."

I'm going to regret this, but I can't help asking, "What do you mean, 'signs'?"

Epatha leans forward again. "If he's dating someone, he'll start worrying about how he looks. He'll probably start dieting or lifting weights. That kind of thing," she says.

I snort. "Lift weights? *Dad*?" This idea is so funny that I laugh out loud. All of a sudden I realize I've been making a big deal out of nothing. "Okay. My dad starts pumping iron, you'll be the first to know. Maybe he'll win the Mr. Universe contest this year."

JoAnn and Al laugh.

Epatha looks slightly offended. "Well, don't say I didn't warn you," she says, popping another lime candy into her mouth, and following that by taking another chomp on a breadstick. "Tastes good together," she explains.

"Lime and garlic?" Jerzey Mae says faintly, clutching her stomach as if she's going to be sick.

I slurp the last bit of my soda just as Cheng comes in to pick me up. "I'd better get home," I say. "Gotta go see if Dad's getting a face-lift or something."

JoAnn howls with laughter; Epatha rolls her eyes.

As Cheng and I walk home, every once in a while my thoughts drift back to what Epatha said. But then I realize how silly I'm being. Epatha's nuts. My dad dating? No way.

Chapter 6

"You're *what*?" I holler.

Dad and I are on the couch. I'm sitting cross-legged at one end, my back propped against the couch's arm. Dad is next to me, turned so he can look straight at me. He clears his throat, then repeats what he just said.

"I'm . . . I've been spending time with a really nice woman," he says, a little faster this time, as if he wants to get it over with.

"You mean, you're . . . like . . . dating someone?"

He nods.

I can't believe it. A few hours earlier, I was laughing my head off at Epatha's dumb idea. Now it turns out she's right.

I stare at him. "You're not getting a face-lift, are you?"

"A what? Of course not. Why would I get a face-lift?" His hands rise to his face, as if he can't control them. He bobs his head to one side, trying to catch a glimpse of himself in the mirror on our wall. "Do you think I need a face-lift?" he asks.

I don't answer. "How long have you been . . . you know?" I ask. I don't even want to say it.

"We've known each other a few months now. Her name is Marjory." His voice softens a little as he says her name. I want to throw up. "She's really nice, Terrel. I think you'll like her. And she would love to meet you. Do you think that would be all right?"

My head's swimming. It's as if everything I depended on weren't dependable at all anymore, as if the floor under me had turned to Jell-O and were all wobbly instead of strong and secure.

I'm suddenly aware of how quiet it is in the living room. I can hear the sounds of Danny's computer game coming from his bedroom, and Cheng's music thumping through the ceiling.

Dad's waiting for me to answer. He looks uncomfortable. Well, fine. He should.

I stall. "Does she have any kids?"

He shakes his head. "But she has a niece who spends every Saturday with her." He starts to say more but stops himself.

I barely notice. Now I'm remembering the way Cheng looked at Tai when Dad came out of his room the night of his "appointment."

"The boys already know, don't they?" I ask.

He nods. "Cheng guessed. I asked them not to say anything to you until you and I could talk about it," Dad says, "since you're a bit younger than they are."

Now, this makes me mad. I run the whole house, and I'm the last to find out what's going on? But underneath the mad, I'm mostly scared—scared that things might *really* change now.

We sit for a minute in silence, until Dad moves closer and puts his arm around me. "Terrel, the fact that I'm dating—it doesn't mean that I love you any less," he says.

My eyes prickle a little, so I blink hard and cross my arms over my chest.

He continues. "Sometimes it's just nice to have another grown-up to talk with."

I look for a good argument. "Danny's twenty-two. He's a grown-up, kind of. Why don't you talk to him?"

Dad smiles. "I'm not very interested in talking about weight lifting or computer games, I'm afraid."

He has a point. As if to illustrate this, we hear an explosion and a yowl of frustration from Danny's room; Danny must have crashed his Super Freeway 3000 race car again.

"You don't need to worry," Dad says. "Marjory and I are just getting to know each other. We aren't going to run off and get married next week or anything."

"Get *married*?"

"Or maybe ever," he adds hastily. "We're taking it slow. I think you'll feel better after you meet her and see how nice she is. What do you say? Maybe we can all do something fun together."

I think about this. It's always best to face the enemy head-on and know what you're dealing with. And I might as well do it on my home turf. "Grocery shopping?" I ask.

He looks a little surprised, but says, "Of course. I'm sure she'd love to come grocery shopping with us."

Good. One minute in that store with me and she'll see that I've got everything under control. And maybe Dad will realize that we don't need some stupid lady around.

Or better yet, she won't want to come at all. What kind of nut goes on a date at a supermarket? I am probably the only person in the world who would like that.

Feeling happier, I nod. "Okay. Maybe she can come shopping with us. Someday."

Dad stands up, bends over, and kisses the top of my head. "Don't worry, Terrel," he says. "You'll like her."

We'll see about that.

Chapter 7

When I told Dad it might be okay for Marjory to come shopping with us *someday*, I meant a long time from now, like next summer. No point in rushing things. But here it is, only a few days later, and we're in the grocery store waiting for Marjory.

She's ten minutes late already. I hate it when people are late. It's not very organized of them. I feel stupid as we all just stand there in a group by the vending machines waiting for her to show up. At least it's not our whole family: Danny and Cheng are busy, so it's just Dad, Edward, Tai, and me. But the store manager has already asked us twice if he can help us with something. Dad says no but doesn't go into details. I guess he doesn't want anyone to know he takes women on grocery-store dates.

Now Marjory's *twelve* minutes late. Just as I start to hope she won't show up at all, Dad's face lights up and he waves. A tall woman with dark skin and bright pink fingernails walks into the store. She has straight, shiny black hair pulled back into a ponytail. Gold hoops dangle from her earlobes. She looks a little familiar, but I'm not sure why.

"Marjory!" Dad says, a little flustered. He starts to hug her, but then reconsiders and ends up sticking out his hand awkwardly for a handshake. She shakes his hand as though this were the most normal thing in the world. Although I definitely do not plan to like Marjory, there's a little part of me that is grateful to her for not making Dad look silly.

Marjory turns to us. "Let me guess— Edward?"

Edward blushes and holds out his hand, which she shakes.

"And Tai, right?"

Tai nods. Both he and Edward are just staring at Marjory. She is pretty, I guess, but it's still annoying to have them gaping at her like fish.

She turns to me. "And you must be Terrel," she says. Her eyes are warm. "Your dad has told me so much about you." She holds her hand out to me. I shake it, then let it go really quickly.

"So," she says, brightly. "Your dad tells me you're a grocery-shopping expert. I can't wait to see you in action."

I'm pleased in spite of myself.

"Shall we get started?" she says. Dad gets a cart. I pull out my binder and look at the list.

"Okay," I say as we walk past the frozen foods. "Cereal is the first stop. While we do that, Edward, you go get bananas," I say.

Marjory peers over my shoulder at the list. "Frozen corn, huh? I'll grab that," she says, heading toward a freezer case.

"No!" I say. It comes out a little loud, and Dad gives me a warning look. "I mean, if we get it now, it'll thaw before we go home. We get frozen stuff last."

"Of course," Marjory says. "That's very smart."

"Bananas!" I say to Edward again. "And Tai, you go get toothpaste."

But instead of running off the way they usually do, they just stand there.

"Aw, Terrel," Edward says, "why don't we just all go around together?"

Why aren't they listening to me? Maybe they just want to hang around and stare at Marjory. Or maybe they don't want a little kid ordering them around in front of company. Whatever it is, it's endangering our shopping mission.

Dad sees I'm getting frustrated. "Edward, Tai, go on," he says.

They head off, thank goodness.

"So, where are we heading?" Marjory asks. "Cereal? I think it's faster if you go this way." She starts to pull the cart toward the front of the store.

I yank back on the cart. "We can't go that way, because we need to get juice." So far, this

whole Dad-having-a-girlfriend thing stinks.

Dad points the cart toward the juice aisle and says quickly, "Terrel, Marjory works for the Ballet Company of New York. Isn't that interesting?"

"Oh," I say. This actually *is* interesting, but I try to hide it. I hunt for the right brand of cornflakes as she answers.

"Yes," she says. "I work in their advertising

and promotion department." She comes over and helps me get the cornflakes, since they're on a high shelf. I guess she's not totally useless.

Edward comes back with bananas, followed by Tai with the toothpaste. Marjory starts asking them questions about school and stuff as I check things off on my shopping list. Once the boys start doing what they're supposed to do, and Marjory learns not to get in the way, the shopping gets done. It takes longer than usual, which is annoying, because I'm trying to break our old speed record (thirty-two items in eight minutes). But it could be worse.

After we check our stuff out, Dad invites Marjory to come back home with us. She says she can't.

"Good," I say under my breath. Tai hears me and steps on my toe.

"But I have an idea," Margory says. "How would you and Terrel like to see *Sleeping*

Beauty? The Ballet Company of London is doing it in our theater. I can get you tickets."

Tickets for *Sleeping Beauty*? The glorious, Important Ballet *Sleeping Beauty* that costs a billion trillion bucks?

"That would be really great," I say. I can't help myself—I smile big. Marjory smiles back.

"You boys are welcome to come, too, if you'd like," she says.

Edward shakes his head hastily. "No thanks," he says. He thinks ballet is stupid.

"How about you, Tai? Or is ballet not your thing, either?" Marjory says.

"Nope," Tai says. "But thank you, anyway," he adds quickly after Dad clears his throat.

"No worries," Marjory says. "I have a niece who lives in Florida who can't stand ballet. But my other niece, the one who spends every Saturday with me, loves it." She turns to me. "In fact, Terrel, your dad probably told you, but . . ."

She's interrupted by a big crash—Dad has accidentally run the shopping cart into a guardrail in the parking lot. This is not like him. He is usually an excellent shopping-cart driver, which is why that's his job on our grocery-store trips. But he seems nervous all of a sudden.

"So, Marjory, thank you very much for coming with us today," he says quickly. "And we can talk about the ballet later, right?"

She looks surprised, but says that would be fine. She offers to give us a ride home with the groceries, but it would be hard to have all of us crammed in her little car, so we say we'll walk, like we usually do.

Then there's another awkward moment. Dad and Marjory are standing next to each other, and for a second there I'm afraid they're going to kiss, which would be totally disgusting. Edward and Tai are staring at them too, probably thinking the same thing.

But they don't. Dad just says he'll call her soon, and she says it was nice to meet all of us, then gets into her car. Phew.

Dad waves as she drives out of the parking lot. Then he turns to us. "Well, what do you think?" he asks.

"She's nice," Tai says. Edward nods, shifting the two grocery bags he's carrying.

We start walking home, kind of slowly, since we all have bags to carry. "Did you like her, Terrel?" Dad asks.

I consider this. She is definitely not a grocery-shopping genius. But I am excited about seeing *Sleeping Beauty*. My stomach does a happy little jump at the idea of being in a big theater, watching famous dancers perform a Very Important Ballet.

"She's okay," I say finally. "But maybe grocery shopping should be a family-only thing."

Dad seems satisfied with this. "It's a deal," he says.

Chapter 8

When we get home, there are seven messages from Epatha on our answering machine. Seriously. *Seven.*

After we've put the groceries away, I call her back. She answers the phone with, "Well? Well? Well?"

"How did you know it was me?" I ask suspiciously.

"Caller ID, *ragazza pazza*," she replies. "What's she like?"

I know she's talking about Marjory. "I don't know. Okay, I guess," I say. "She was late. And she is terrible at grocery shopping. Even worse than you." Epatha came with us once and helped us pack up the shopping bags. When I wasn't watching, she put a bunch of ripe bananas at the bottom of the bag, then put a gallon of apple juice right on top of them.

Epatha exhales impatiently. "I don't care how she shops! What does she look like? Is she nice?"

"She's pretty, I guess," I say, sitting down on the couch. "And I guess she's nice."

I can almost hear Epatha bouncing around on the other end of the phone. "Details! I want details!"

"She was exactly twelve minutes late," I say.

"*Arrrrrgh!*" she says. I have to hold the phone away from my ear. "Did she and your dad hold hands or kiss or anything?"

"No!" I say. Great—now I feel all shaky and weird again. Eager to get Epatha off this subject, I add, "But she's getting Dad and me tickets for *Sleeping Beauty*."

"You've got to be kidding me! How? Is she rich?"

I explain about Marjory's job. Thankfully, this gets Epatha off the Dad subject and onto *Sleeping Beauty*.

"*¡Qué suerte tienes!* Lucky you!" she says.

After I hang up, I lie on my bed and stare at the ceiling. The ballet will be great. But I'm not exactly feeling lucky at the moment. I close my eyes and wish as hard as I can that my family will stay exactly the same. If I'm really lucky, that's what will happen.

Do things get any better? No, they do not. Monday after school, I'm in the kitchen watching Tai crunch through a mammoth bowl of cornflakes. "Hurry up," I tell him. "You need to take me down to Red Rose Cleaners so we can pick up Dad's shirts."

Tai shovels another spoonful of cereal into his mouth. "*Dmnt nrrdf dd*," he says.

60

I swear. Brothers have no manners. "What?" I say, putting my hands on my hips. "Want to try that again?"

He swallows. "Don't need to," he says, motioning to the fridge.

The dry-cleaning pickup slip is gone.

"Marjory was over here last night when you were asleep," he says. "She noticed the slip and says the dry-cleaning place is right by where she works," Tai says. "She's going to pick up the shirts and save us the trip." He scoops up another mound of cereal.

I exhale in frustration. I'd planned my schedule today around that trip. Now there's a half-hour hole in my day where the walk to the dry cleaners is supposed to be.

Tai notices the deadly look on my face. "She's just trying to be nice, T.," he says. "Doing us a favor."

"If she wants to do us a favor, she can stop messing with the way our house runs," I say.

"Whoa." Tai puts down his spoon. "What's the matter?"

I don't answer. Instead, I flip through my binder, turning the pages hard. "Don't forget you have to take your science project to school tomorrow," I tell him. "Unless Little Miss Marjory has already done that, too."

I slam the binder and go into my room. Maybe it's good I have an extra half hour today. I think I need to be annoyed for at least that long.

That night I remind Dad that we need to make a quick trip to the grocery store to get peanut butter and beans. The midweek trips are always just him and me, not all my brothers, too. It's fun to get to be alone with Dad.

"Oh . . ." he says. "Uh . . ."

"What?"

"Marjory and I had lunch today. We were

right by the supermarket, so we picked up the things we need. I checked your binder first," he says quickly. "Just to make sure."

I run to the lowest cupboard and open it up. Sure enough, there's stuff in there. And it's all in the wrong place.

Dad comes into the kitchen. "Marjory helped put some of the things away," he explains, apologetically.

I don't say anything. I start pulling things out so I can put them away correctly. "I can't reach the peanut butter when it's up there," I say, pointing to one of the high cupboards. My voice sounds weird—high and strained, as if it might crack into a million pieces. "I *need* to be able to reach the peanut butter."

Dad quickly starts helping me pull things out of the cupboard.

"Don't worry, sweetheart," he says. "We can put everything back in the right place. Marjory and I were talking, and I guess I wasn't paying attention. She was just trying to help."

"We don't *need* her help," I say, slamming cans of beans on the counter.

"Terrel, wait," he says. I turn to face him because he expects me to, but I don't want to look at him, because I'm so upset. Instead I stare over his shoulder at the lumpy orange refrigerator magnet I made in kindergarten.

"You do so much to help us around the house," he says. "It makes me feel bad. You're just a little girl." He looks sad.

"I'm almost *nine*," I say. "And I *like* organizing stuff. And grocery shopping," I add.

"I know, but aren't there other things you might like better?" he asks. "If someday . . . well, if someday there were two grown-ups around, you wouldn't have all that responsibility," he says, tapping his finger gently on my household binder.

I pull the binder away. I want to tell him

that I *like* that responsibility, just as I like grocery shopping. I'm good at it. It makes me feel important. My dad and my brothers need me, because I make everything run smoothly. If I weren't doing it, they wouldn't need me at all. I'd just be a stupid little kid.

I want to tell Dad this, but I don't know how. So I turn back to the cupboard and start loading the groceries back inside, in exactly the right places.

Chapter 9

"We have ballet tickets for tomorrow night!" Dad says as he comes home one evening, a big grin on his face. Despite all the Marjory Issues, I am looking forward to the ballet. After all the cupboard rearranging and dry-cleaning interfering, I feel like she owes me.

Dad holds out the envelope, and I look at the tickets. Yep—tomorrow! I carefully tuck them away in my binder for safekeeping, since Dad's been a bit scatterbrained lately.

The next night after dinner, I put on my red and black dress and some tights.

"You look really nice, T.," Cheng says from the couch, where he's watching an old movie.

Dad rushes out in his suit. "The tickets!" he says, checking his pockets. "Where—"

I hand them to him.

"What *would* we do without you?" he says, kissing the top of my head.

I grin.

Danny's head pops out of his room. "Have a good time, you guys," he says.

"Yeah—have fun at the bal-*llaaaaaaayy*," Edward says, doing a leap, followed by an awkward turn, which sends him reeling into the coffee table.

"We will," Dad says.

We catch a cab right away. The cabdriver is humming to himself, and warm air is blasting through the heating vents. It feels good just sitting here with my dad. It's been a long time since we did something special together, just the two of us. I press my head against the smooth coldness of the window. Multicolored Christmas lights shine through the night,

their colors reflected on the fluffy white snow. I know by tomorrow all the snow will be trampled and muddy, but right now it's beautiful.

A few minutes later, we pull up in front of the theater. A crowd of well-dressed people is gathered in front. A line snakes away from the box office. Ushers in red uniforms are stationed at the doorways, tearing tickets and letting people in.

We walk in the door. I've never been in a big, fancy theater like this one. All I can say is "Wow." A huge glass chandelier dangles above the lobby. People are hanging out, sipping champagne, and talking.

"Our seats are up on the next level," Dad says, pointing me toward a sweeping stairway.

I walk up, my feet sinking into the red carpet with each step. At the top of the stairs there's a landing; a bar stretches along the back wall, and people are lined up to buy drinks and candy. There's a mirror on the wall behind the bar that reflects the bartenders with their white shirts and black bow ties, making it look like there are twice as many of them as there really are.

There's a door into the main theater on either side of the bar. The restrooms are behind us; I make a note of this in case I have to go at intermission. The good thing about being a kid is that you can move a lot faster than grown-ups if you have to do a bathroom dash; and if you're all dressed up, like I am now, they think you're cute even when you accidentally crash into them.

Dad buys me a fancy souvenir program. Then I crane my neck to look at our tickets, which Dad is holding in his hand. "We're on the left, so we go in there," I say, starting to walk toward one of the doors.

"I think we should wait out here for Marjory," he says.

I turn around. "What?" I ask.

"Oh, Terrel," he says, seeing my expression. "Didn't you know she was coming with us?"

Stupid me. Of *course* Marjory's coming. How could I have not figured that out? "Uh, no. I knew," I say, trying to cover up the fact that I'm upset.

But Dad can tell. "Honey, I'm sorry. I just

assumed you knew it would be the three of us. I should have told you." He glances around, trying to spot Marjory in the sea of people. "But you do like her, don't you?" he asks.

I'm saved from answering. "Hi, there!" Marjory comes up behind Dad. She's wearing a pink dress and a tan coat. She smiles warmly at me and pats Dad on the shoulder.

"Sorry, I'm a little late," she says.

I give Dad a meaningful look—does he really want to date some lady who never shows up on time?—but he's looking at Marjory.

"We should go in," I say loudly. "It's almost time for the ballet to start."

Marjory looks at her watch. "We still have ten minutes. And we need to wait for my niece. She's still in the restroom."

"Your niece?" Dad says. He looks like he just got a bad case of indigestion.

"Didn't I mention she was coming?"

Marjory asks. "She . . . ah, there she is!"

She waves to someone over my shoulder. I turn around.

Standing there, in a dark green velvet dress, is Tiara Girl.

Chapter 10

Tiara Girl is wearing a tiara (surprise!) with dark green stones that match her dress. She stares at me with narrowed eyes. I glare back at her.

"April, you know Terrel, I'm sure," Marjory says. "You two are in the same ballet class, right?"

Tiara Girl nods. "Hi," she says.

"Hi," I reply.

"And this is Mr. Liu," Marjory motions to my dad.

Dad is trying to smile, but he still looks sick.

Marjory touches Dad's shoulder. "Are you all right?" she asks.

He nods.

"Let's go in, shall we?" Marjory says.

"You go on," he says. "We'll find a drinking fountain first."

As Marjory and Tiara Girl walk into the theater, Dad pulls me aside and whispers, "Terrel, I am so sorry. I had no idea Marjory's niece would be here."

"You *knew* Tiara Girl was her niece?" I say. I can feel my eyes bulging. "And you didn't even *tell* me?"

He looks apologetic. "When you told me you didn't care for April . . ."

"She's a pain in the neck!" I say.

". . . I thought it would be better if you got to know Marjory first. I certainly didn't mean to spring it on you like this. I . . ." He runs out of words.

This is why I can't wait to grow up. Even if you're a very organized kid, adults can do things that totally mess up your life.

I shake my head. "We'd better go in." I can see Dad is still upset.

But not half as upset as I am.

We enter the theater. An usher shows us to our seats. They're in the front row of the loge, which is a fancy word for "balcony." They're great seats, even better because no tall guy or lady with a huge hat can sit in front of me. I would be having a great time if it weren't for the fact that my life is turning into a horror story before my eyes.

"Do you girls want to sit together?" Marjory asks.

"No!" Tiara Girl, Dad, and I say in unison.

"I mean, why don't you two sit in the middle, so you can talk," Tiara Girl says, sweetly.

Marjory looks surprised, but we arrange ourselves so that the grown-ups are in between us.

My brain is swirling. Maybe I'm having a nightmare. Maybe this isn't really happening. Marjory leafs through the program and points things out to Dad. Dad keeps looking over at me like I might explode at any second.

I lean forward a little and peer down the row, to find that Tiara Girl's doing the same thing. We glower at each other, then lean back in our seats.

How could Dad do this to me? Dating someone is bad enough, but dating Tiara Girl's aunt? What if he and Marjory end up getting married? What if I have to spend holidays and vacations with Tiara Girl?

Fortunately, the theater lights start to dim. The musicians in the orchestra pit, which is down below the front of the stage, tune their instruments. Everyone claps as the conductor enters. She lifts her baton, the music starts, and soon the red stage curtains part.

For the next hour I don't think about anything but ballet. The sets are gorgeous. So are the costumes. And the dancing is totally amazing. I didn't know ballet could look like this. The women in the corps de ballet move exactly in unison—not just kind-of, sort-of together, the way we do in class. The men bound across the stage like stags leaping across a field. When the princess and prince dance together, it's so beautiful my heart nearly stops. The music is full of sadness and long-ing. The dancers come together, then break away from each other, then come together again. When I fall in love, a million years from now, I want it to feel the same way they look.

The curtain falls, and I clap so hard my hands hurt. But when the houselights come up at intermission, I remember where I am— and whom I'm with.

"What do you think, Terrel?" Marjory asks, leaning across Dad. "Really good, huh?"

I nod.

"That's really a lovely dress you're wearing," she says to me.

I can see this makes Tiara Girl mad, which is fine with me.

"You said you liked my dress, too," Tiara Girl says.

Marjory looks a little surprised. "Yes, of course I do, sweetheart."

"Do you want to get up to stretch your

legs?" Dad asks me. I think he's trying to get me out of there until intermission's over.

I watch, out of the corner of my eye. I want to be wherever Tiara Girl's not. She looks as if she's starting to stand up, so I say, "No."

"I need to use the restroom," Dad says, apologetically.

"That's fine; I'll stay here with the girls," Marjory says.

But she doesn't. After Dad leaves, a woman a few rows back calls out to Marjory, and Marjory goes back to chat with her. And I'm stranded with Tiara Girl.

Now that the grown-ups are out of earshot, Tiara Girl and I can be openly hostile. After a minute, she scoots over and sits in Dad's seat. "So, when did your stupid dad start going out with my aunt?"

I glare at her. "You call my dad stupid one more time and I'll whack that tiara right off your head," I say. "And I'm not sure how long. Did you know about this?"

She snorts. "Of course not. Do you think I would have agreed to come if I'd known you'd be here?"

I love how she says, "agreed to come," as if she's doing everyone a favor by being here. Some favor. I'm sure all the London ballet stars are thrilled she's here.

"Well, what are we going to do?" she says.

"Hope they break up soon," I say.

She stands up to go back to her seat. "Well, if your dad's anything like you, she'll definitely get sick of him fast," she says.

I pop up to go thump her, but just then Dad and Marjory both return.

Dad looks horrified that we had been left alone together. *I'm sorry,* he mouths when they're not looking.

"You girls having a nice chat?" Marjory asks.

"Uh-huh," I say. Tiara Girl smiles a big, fake smile.

The second half of the show is as good as the first, but Tiara Girl's gotten under my skin and I don't enjoy it as much. By the time the curtain drops for the last time, I've decided that something definitely needs to be done. But what?

After the show, we all walk down the stairs to the lobby together. "Would you two like to go out and have some ice cream with us?" Marjory asks.

"It's a school night," I say. "I should be in bed already."

"Well, it's a special day," she says, as Dad helps her into her coat. "I think it's fine to stay up late once in a while."

I bet Dad would like to spend more time with Marjory. I'll bet he wants me to say yes, but I feel mean, and the last thing I want to do is hang out with Tiara Girl for another hour. I force a big yawn. "I'm *really* tired," I say.

"Maybe another time," Marjory says. She puts her hand on his arm. The hair on the back of my neck rises.

"Sure," I say. There will be another time, I think, over my dead body.

Chapter 11

Even though Dad says he and Marjory aren't rushing things, it sure seems to me like they're rushing. Thursday night he mentions that he had lunch with her. And Friday night he dashes off, smelling like pine again. He comes back later that night in a good mood. I even see him dancing around the kitchen with a dish towel when he doesn't know I'm watching. This is serious.

I haven't told my friends that Dad's dating Tiara Girl's aunt. It still stings a little that they didn't get how bad it is that Dad is dating at all. Brenda and I go to the same school, and she knows something's wrong. However, since she wants to be a doctor, she looks at everything from a medical perspective. She thinks my bad mood is due to a vitamin deficiency, and she even told me to ask my dad about getting some multivitamins for kids. But I know my problem isn't too few vitamins; it's too much Marjory.

Saturday morning I get ready for class. I pull on my tights and my leotard. Tai, who wants to be a hairstylist when he grows up, braided my hair last night, and it looks pretty good.

Dad knocks on my door.

"Almost ready?" he asks. He's more dressed up than usual. I know it's because he'll be seeing you-know-who, since it's Saturday and she'll be dropping Tiara Girl off at class. Vomit.

"Yeah," I say. I pull my ballet slippers off the shelf and put them in my bag, then open the door.

"I saw Marjory the other night," he says from the doorway.

I don't say anything.

He clears his throat, then continues. "She was wondering if you and I would like to go to the zoo with her and April next weekend."

"Well, we wouldn't," I say, standing up.

"Now, Terrel," he says. He doesn't look angry. He looks disappointed in me, which is worse. "You know that April stays with Marjory on Saturdays. I'm afraid that sometimes you are just going to need to spend time with her. You don't have to be best friends. . . ."

I laugh a short, sharp laugh.

". . . But you are going to have to figure out how to get along."

I was afraid of this. I guess Dad thinks hanging out with Marjory is more important than me being happy. That's a pretty crummy thing for a parent to think.

I'm trying to figure out what to say when Dad hands me a white box that's tied up with a blue ribbon.

"What's this?" I ask.

"It's a present for you. From Marjory," he adds. "She said it's an early Christmas gift, but that you can open it now."

I untie the ribbon and open the box. Inside is a tiara with sparkly blue stones.

"April really loves her tiaras, so Marjory thought you'd like to have one, too," he says. "I told her blue was your favorite color."

"Wow," I say, looking into the box. "Wow." I wonder if it's too big to flush down the toilet.

Dad looks at his watch. "Why don't you wear it to class?" he says. "I'm sure Marjory would like to see you wearing it."

Here we go again. He doesn't care if *I'd* be happy about wearing it.

I can't even imagine what my friends would say if I walked in wearing a tiara. It would be as if JoAnn came to class wearing a frilly bonnet instead of her baseball cap, or if Brenda showed up with an armload of fashion magazines instead of medical textbooks.

"Dad, I really can't," I say.

He exhales. "Terrel, we're going to be late. Please put the tiara on. We don't want to be rude to Marjory."

I stick the stupid tiara on my head.

"Beautiful," he says. "You look like a princess," he says, opening the door for me. I wish I were a princess. Then I could have Marjory and Tiara Girl tossed into a cold, clammy dungeon forever.

It's deadly cold outside. The snow that has fallen over the last several days has melted and then frozen again, coating the sidewalks with patches of ice. It seems as if every few steps my boots slip and I have to grab on to Dad's arm. The icy snowflakes falling now sting my eyes and face. They are little and mean, just like the way I feel.

As we walk, I keep my head down in case we pass anyone I know. All I have to do is get through the front door of the school. Then I can duck into the bathroom and pull the tiara off my head before anyone sees me. I'll need to put it back on before I leave, but I'll worry about that later.

Finally we get to the ballet school. By some amazing stroke of luck, no one's hanging around outside. I just may get into the building without being noticed.

"Well, 'bye," I say hastily and start to climb the stairs. I hear snow crunching behind me. Dad's climbing the stairs behind me.

"What are you doing?" I ask, a note of panic in my voice. So far the coast is still clear, but someone I know could come along any time.

"I'm just going to the office to pay for this month's classes," he says.

Great. I push open the door and a warm

blast of air hits me in the face. "Have a good class," Dad says. Clearly he's going to stand there watching me until I go into the waiting room. I'm doomed.

I turn and walk in. My friends are all gathered at the far end of the room. As I slowly approach, they stop talking.

"What in the world . . . ?" Epatha asks.

Brenda leaps up and examines the tiara closely, as if it were some big germ that had just landed on my head. "Delirious be must she," she says to the others. Then she feels my forehead. "Do you know your name?" she says, slowly and distinctly, as if I were three years old. "What month is this?"

Jerzey Mae looks scared. Jessica looks worried. Al stares at me in horror.

JoAnn's eyes are about to pop out of her head. "Why?" she asks.

"Present," I manage to croak. "From Tiara Girl's aunt. Dating my dad."

Epatha jumps up, shaking her head wildly. "Oh no. No, no, no. This is just wrong," she says. "Terrel and tiaras, they do *not* go together. You need to get that thing off your head."

"Can't," I say. "Dad's in the office. He might see."

"You'd better sit down," Jessica says. I collapse on the bench.

Tiara Girl and her snotty friend come into the studio. She sees me and immediately stomps over to us.

"Is that one of my tiaras?" she asks, furiously.

"No," I say.

"Then why does it look exactly like mine?" she asks.

"You think I'd steal one of your stinking tiaras?" I yell. "Your dumb aunt gave it to me, and my dad made me wear it. I don't know why he's going out with her, anyway."

Tiara Girl's friend stares at her. "Your aunt is going out with *her* dad?"

Tiara Girl nods curtly.

Her friend blinks. "Well, your aunt sure seems happy lately," she says.

"I don't *care* if my aunt's happy," Tiara Girl says. She gives me a look so ugly that even though I always expect her to be awful, I'm still startled. "I care that it will ruin my life if I have to spend any more time with *her*." She flings her arm out dramatically and points at me.

"Well, I'm not thrilled at the idea of hanging out with you, either, you big, stuck-up cow," I say, my voice rising.

"How dare you call me big, pipsqueak?" she spits.

"Girls!"

Ms. Debbé marches over to us and bangs her walking stick on the floor. We immediately fall silent.

"Is this any way for young ladies to behave? I think it is not." Ms. Debbé pounds the stick again for emphasis. "There will be no fighting in my studio. No name-calling. Ever. Is that understood?"

Tiara Girl and I both nod.

"Now. You will shake hands. Then you will be friends."

Fat chance. But we shake hands. As we do, I see Dad coming out of the office. He sees

Tiara Girl and me shaking hands and looking all chummy. He smiles and waves good-bye.

"Very good. The class, it begins," says Ms. Debbé. She strides regally across the room and starts up the stairs to the studio.

Epatha whispers something to JoAnn, who nods. Then Epatha turns to me. "Okay, girlfriend," she says in a low voice. "We get it now. Dad dating is one thing. Dad dating Tiara Girl's aunt is a whole different ball game."

"You think?" I say irritably, yanking the tiara off my head and throwing it in my bag.

"Don't worry," she says as we walk up the stairs. "We'll help you get out of this. Okay?"

I nod, relieved. Just knowing my friends finally understand makes me feel better. Maybe with their help I can think of a way to get Marjory out of our lives once and for all.

Chapter 12

We line up in rows in the ballet studio—well, all of us except for JoAnn, who sits on the floor by the windows. Al is on my left, and Jessica is on my right. Epatha, Brenda, and Jerzey Mae are behind us.

"Okay, *amigas*," Epatha whispers as Ms. Debbé

starts the music. "Put on your thinking caps—
as long as they don't look like tiaras."

"Grand pliés!" announces Ms. Debbé.
"One . . . two . . . three . . . four."

As we plié up and down, our images are
reflected in the mirror that stretches along
the front of the studio. I can see the looks of
concentration on my friends' faces. Jessica is
gazing off into the distance, and Jerzey Mae's
eyebrows are knitted. I know they don't have
to concentrate that hard to do pliés, so they
must be working on solving my problem.

"Tendus!" Ms. Debbé calls.

"I think you should act like a monster," says Al quietly as we slide our right feet to the side and point our toes. "Turn into 'Terrible Terrel.' Then she won't want to stick around."

I must admit, I do like the sound of Terrible Terrel.

Jessica shakes her head as we switch to our left legs. "That wouldn't be very nice," she says. Jessica is extremely thoughtful and considerate. This is good in everyday life, but bad when you are trying to scare off your dad's girlfriend.

"Now, ladies—please gather to one side. We will now practice jetés," Ms. Debbé says.

We gather on the left side of the room. Two by two, girls leap across the floor while a tinkly piano CD plays. "Leap! . . . and leap!" calls Ms. Debbé. "Straighten the front leg, my dear. Higher, higher. Like you are a lovely deer."

My friends and I all linger near where JoAnn is sitting. "The terrible thing wouldn't work anyway," I say. "Dad would just make me stop acting terrible, then I'd be back where I started."

"So you need to act terrible when she's around but your dad isn't," Epatha says.

"When would I ever be alone with her?" I ask. "It's not like she comes over and lounges around in our house when Dad's not there. Even if she did, she'd probably be too busy messing up our cupboards to notice me being terrible."

"It could happen," Brenda says.

JoAnn leans forward in her chair. "Maybe we could help you be terrible!" she says with sudden enthusiasm. "A terrible kid is bad enough, but a terrible kid with six terrible friends would be even worse."

"Girls!" Ms. Debbé raps her walking stick on the floor. "So much chatter! Please."

Although I still don't see how this is all going to come together, we decide on a plan. We will all think of different ways to be terrible (all except Jessica, who couldn't be terrible if her life depended on it, and Jerzey Mae, who is too high-strung to be terrible). Brenda remembers seeing an old movie where two kids try to scare their dad's girlfriend off during a camping trip. She's going to watch that and take notes, since she likes doing research. The others will just think of terrible things on their own.

And I'll try to find some way for us to be alone with Marjory. I still don't know if that will happen, but it's such a relief to have my friends on my side again that I'm willing to be hopeful.

"Watch and wait," Epatha says, as she and I prepare to jeté across the room. "We'll get that tiara out of your life in no time."

Chapter 13

Miraculously, we get our big chance just two days later. I'm sitting at home when Dad calls.

"Marjory and I are going out to dinner tonight," he says. "She's coming over at five thirty, but I have an important meeting that's been delayed, so I'll be late." He sounds worried.

"Can't you call her?" I ask.

"I think she is the only person in New York without a cell phone," he says. "And she said she was going to be out running errands this afternoon. Can you do me a favor? Can you please apologize for me when she gets there, and entertain her till I get back?"

Entertain her? "What am I supposed to

do—juggle or something?" I ask.

"Just get her something to drink, and chat with her. Please, Terrel. You and Cheng are going to be the only ones home, and you know he has a chemistry exam tomorrow. It will only be for half an hour or so."

I quickly check my organizational binder, since Dad has been known to be wrong. But this time he's right: Edward has basketball practice; Tai has chorus practice; and Danny's at work this afternoon. Sigh. But then it feels as if a jolt of electricity were going through my body. This is it—my golden opportunity to be Terrible Terrel!

"Okay," I say, much more enthusiastically. "I'll entertain her, all right."

I hang up and look at the clock: four o'clock. I don't have much time.

I call Epatha, who says she'll call everyone else. Luckily, one of Epatha's big sisters owes her a favor. Epatha is *always* catching her older sisters sneaking out to meet their boyfriends. So, her sisters do pretty much anything Epatha wants in return for her keeping her mouth shut. Epatha and one of her sisters will go around and pick the other girls up. Since Cheng is twenty, he's old enough so that we can honestly say a grown-up will be here, even if he's locked in his room studying chemistry.

At five o'clock, the doorbell rings and my friends come in. Al, Brenda, Epatha, and JoAnn have brought the stuff they need for their most terrible ideas. Jessica and Jerzey Mae have come along for moral support.

"Okay, troops," I say, "what have we got?"

Epatha pulls out a fake ice cube with a spider inside it. "A spider in a plastic ice cube," she says. "Put it in her drink and she'll pass out."

"She's not the only one," Al says. She runs over to steady Jerzey Mae, who looks like she's about to pass out herself.

"Ooh, good one," JoAnn says, admiring the spider's hairy legs.

"It's not a real spider, is it?" asks Jessica in horror. This is not because she's afraid of spiders. It's because if she thought some company were killing spiders to stick them in fake ice cubes, she'd report them to the Society for the Prevention of Cruelty to Multilegged Creatures.

"Plastic," Epatha says quickly. "Plastic spider."

Jessica heaves a sigh of relief.

"Next?" I ask.

"Stink bomb," JoAnn says triumphantly, pulling out a small bottle. "I was at a friend's house, and her brother set one off. It stank to high heaven. He gave me one."

I nod approvingly.

Al shows us a CD. "Loud music," she says. "Grown-ups hate loud music. And this CD is terrible. My neighbor across the hall had it, and his mom made him throw it out. I pulled it out of the trash bin," she says, pleased with herself.

"And how about you?" I ask Brenda.

She takes something out of a bag. Everyone screams, even me.

"Human-heart model," she says. "It comes apart, but I used some modeling clay to stick it together temporarily. We can hide it in her purse or something."

The heart looks very realistic, red and gory. Little tubes that are supposed to be blood vessels are hanging out of it.

I smile with satisfaction. "You guys are the best," I say. "No way would anyone put up with all this stuff. She'll be out the door in two seconds flat."

We get everything ready. When the doorbell rings, a thrill of excitement goes through my body. Good-bye, Marjory. Good-bye, Tiara Girl.

"Who is it?" I ask through the intercom. When Marjory responds, I buzz to let her in. A few seconds later, there's a knock, and I open our front door.

"Hi, Terrel," Marjory says. She looks genuinely pleased to see me. Not for long!

"Hi," I say. "Dad says he's sorry, but he's going to be late. You're supposed to come in, though."

"Oh," she says, "all right. It'll give us a chance to get to know each other a little better, huh?"

I smile sweetly.

Marjory comes into the living room, where my friends are waiting. I introduce everyone. "Would you like something to drink?" Epatha asks, her restaurant experience taking over before I can say anything.

Marjory sits on the couch and puts her briefcase down on the floor beside her. "Maybe a cup of tea," she says.

"How about something nice and cold?" Epatha suggests. "It's kind of, uh, hot in here." She fans herself with her hand as if it were the middle of July instead of early December.

Marjory smiles. "All right. Ice water?"

"Good choice!" Epatha says, bounding out of the room. She returns with a glass of water. She hands it to Marjory, and we all watch intently.

Marjory lifts the glass to her lips, then puts it back down. "Well, my goodness," she says.

"There seems to be a spider in here." She plucks the ice cube out with her pink fingernails and examines it under the light by the couch. "Not sure what kind, though. It's not a brown recluse, or a garden spider." She turns the ice cube upside down to look more closely. "I used to love spiders when I was a girl," she says. "Entomology was one of my favorite classes in college. You girls know what that is?" She looks around at us, smiling brightly.

"The study of insects," Brenda says in a dull voice.

"Of course, spiders aren't technically insects, are they?" Marjory says. "Insects only have six legs. Still, I like spiders anyway. Hello, handsome!" she says to the ice cube.

Well, that sure didn't work. I sneak a meaningful glance to JoAnn. She moves her head slightly in acknowledgment, then says, "Excuse me. I gotta get a drink of water, too."

We sit in silence as she dashes into the

kitchen to set off the stink bomb. There's a soft popping sound, and then a horrible odor slowly trickles into the living room. It smells like a combination of rotten eggs and dog poop. I see my  friends' eyes start to water. How could such a big stink come out of such a little bottle?

Marjory wrinkles her nose. "Do you girls smell something?" she asks. "I wonder if you have a gas leak." She jumps up and goes into the kitchen just as JoAnn comes out, looking slightly guilty.

As soon as Marjory is out of view, we all grab our noses and gag. "Man, oh, man," Al says. Her voice sounds funny, because she doesn't want to let go of her nose. "That's one putrid smell."

"It's a stink bomb," JoAnn says defensively through her nose. "It's supposed to smell. It's supposed to gross Marjory out so she leaves."

"Unfortunately, you forgot that all of us have to smell it, too," says Epatha.

"Man. This is worse than all of my brothers' gym shoes combined," I say. I pick up a throw pillow from the couch and breathe through it. It smells like dust, but that's sure better than the stink wafting through the house. Jerzey Mae slowly leans her head against Jessica's shoulder, and I wonder if she might really pass out this time.

"Where *is* the stink bomb?" Epatha asks.

JoAnn's eyes widen. "Oh, no. I left it right on the floor. She's gonna see it."

Marjory comes out. "Well, it's not a gas leak," she says, walking over to the living room window and opening it wide. "Actually, it smells to me like the stink bombs we used to set off when I was a kid. Terrel, do you have any crazy neighbors around here who might do that?"

"Uh . . . I'm not sure," I say. "Maybe."

Marjory sits back down. "Well, don't worry," she says. "The smell will be gone in a minute." She looks around at us all holding our noses and laughs. "Come on, girls. Is it really that bad? I guess I'm lucky I still have a bit of a cold. I caught it three weeks ago, and my sense of smell still hasn't completely come back."

It figures. No wonder Dad's aftershave doesn't suffocate her.

Clearly, it's time for the double whammy.

"Want to listen to some music?" Al asks.

"Sure," says Marjory. "What do you have?"

"Just a little something I brought from home. It's one of my favorites." Al walks over to the CD player and puts in her disc. As she does, Brenda excuses herself, saying she has to go to the bathroom.

Epatha waits till Brenda's gone, then, in a loud voice, asks Marjory, "So, you work for the Ballet Company of New York?"

"Yes, I do," Marjory replies.

As Epatha asks Marjory questions about her job, Brenda sneaks back into the room on all fours. She crawls behind the couch and sticks the human-heart model down right beside Marjory's briefcase, then crawls back out of the room.

Al turns on the CD. "We all like loud music," she says. "Really loud." She cranks the volume up.

Al's right—the CD is awful. It sounds like some guy screaming while he's scratching his nails against a thousand chalkboards. The throbbing bass beat feels like a stake being pounded into my head. All of my friends look like they're in agony, too. I can see Jerzey Mae trying to resist the temptation to cover her ears. She finally sits on her hands and scrunches up her face as if she were trying to disappear.

The only person who seems to be enjoying

the music is Marjory. She's nodding her head in rhythm to the pounding bass. "It's got a good beat," she says, yelling so that we can hear her over the scratching and screeching. "Anyone want to dance?"

She gets up and starts bouncing around as if she's having the best time of her life. She pulls Epatha and Jessica up and tries to get them to dance with her.

"Come on, ladies!" she says. "Let's get down!"

Finally I can't stand it any longer. I run over and turn off the CD. "I forgot," I say. "My brother's studying. I don't want to disturb him."

"Ah," Marjory says sympathetically. "That's very considerate of you, Terrel."

We sit in silence for a minute. "I was telling you about my job," Marjory says. "I have some pictures from the rehearsals for *Sleeping Beauty* with me. Would you like to see them?"

"Yes," says Jerzey Mae, almost drooling. The other girls look interested, too.

Marjory bends over to get her bag, and her hand brushes against the heart. She bends over to take a look, then picks it up and puts it in her lap.

"Well, I've heard of someone who left his heart in San Francisco, but not someone who left his heart in my briefcase," she says lightly. She turns the heart around and examines it. "Very interesting. I can never remember which are the ventricles and which are the atria."

Brenda eagerly jumps up to point out which chambers of the heart are which. Epatha and I exchange a defeated look. Clearly, every single one of our ideas has flopped. Now Marjory may be even more eager to come over, seeing as she likes spiders and hearts and horrible music so much. I slump backward on the couch.

"I guess we'd better be going," Epatha says after Brenda finishes giving her anatomy lecture.

"You girls okay on your own?" Marjory asks with surprise.

Epatha nods. "My sister's waiting in the coffee shop downstairs." The other girls stand up silently. Marjory stands, too.

"It was so nice to meet you," she says, shaking hands with each one of them. "I hope I'll get to spend time with you all again."

They nod. "'Bye, T.," they each say as they trudge out the door.

"Your friends seem like really lovely girls," Marjory says, as soon as we're alone.

"Hello?" a voice calls from the hallway. Dad appears in the doorway. "Hello, Marjory! Hi, sweetheart." He stomps the snow off his boots. "I'm so sorry I was late," he tells Marjory.

"Terrel, did I see your friends leaving?"

Marjory smiles at him. "No problem. Terrel and her friends were very good hostesses. We had a lovely time, didn't we, Terrel?"

She's looking right at me, but she doesn't look mad, even though she has every right to be. We were not very good hostesses. In fact, we may have been the worst hostesses in the world. Some other woman would probably have told Dad about all the rotten things we did the second he walked in.

"Uh-huh," I mumble.

"Where would you like to go for dinner?" Dad asks Marjory.

She stands up and walks toward the door. "*Hmm*. I don't know. How about somewhere quiet?" she says. "I've had kind of a noisy day."

She looks over her shoulder at me and winks.

Chapter 14

"Well, that was some great plan," I say.

We're all back at Bella Italia on the following Tuesday after class, slumped around our favorite table. The restaurant's nearly empty, but the smell of pizza baking drifts through the air. I inhale deeply. It's going to take a lot of good smells to get rid of the memory of that stink bomb.

Al shakes her head from side to side. "Marjory *liked* that music? She has to be crazy."

"She was very interested in the structure of the heart, though," Brenda says. "She remembered the basic way the blood flows through the heart, just not the actual names for the chambers." She says this as though it were clearly a point in Marjory's favor.

Epatha's mom sits down at a table on the other side of the restaurant. She takes something out of an envelope, unfolds it, reads it, and smiles.

"Your mom looks happy," I say to Epatha.

Epatha rolls her eyes. "Papa writes her a love letter every month. She always gets all sappy when she reads them. Then she carries them around with her and reads them a bunch more times. It's sickening—*repulsivo*," she says, after a hard slurp on her straw.

"Why's he writing her a letter when he can just holler out of the kitchen at her?" Al asks.

"Because writing a letter is different from hollering at someone, silly," Jessica says. "I think it's sweet."

"It's so romantic," Jerzey Mae says, as if she wished someone would write her a love letter.

I wonder if in a few years Marjory will be walking around our apartment reading some mushy letter from my dad and making me sick.

That's when I have my latest brilliant idea.

"That's it!" I say. "Dad needs to write Marjory a letter."

"A love letter?" Jerzey asks. "I thought you wanted them to break up."

"No," I explain. My brain feels like it's clearing after being in a fog for days. "An *anti*love letter. A letter telling her he doesn't want to go out with her anymore."

My friends stare at me as if I were crazy. "But your dad likes her," Brenda says. "Why would he write a letter like that?"

"*He* wouldn't," I explain patiently. "*We* would."

All of a sudden they get it. "We write the letter . . ." says Al.

"And mail it . . ." says JoAnn.

"And voilà, no more Marjory," finishes Epatha. "Not bad, T.!"

Brenda nods thoughtfully. "Printer and computer a need we'll," she says.

Epatha shakes her head. "Not for an important letter like this," she says. "You can't just send someone a printed letter to break up with them. That would be harsh. It has to be handwritten."

Since Epatha reads her older sisters' magazines, we don't question her authority about dating stuff.

"Who has the best handwriting?" she asks.

"Jerzey Mae," says JoAnn immediately.

Jerzey Mae looks pleased, if a little embarrassed. "I have nice stationery, too," she says.

Right then, a strange feeling comes over me. As much as I want to dislike Marjory, she *was* actually really cool about the way we all behaved when she came over. I hate to admit it, but she seems like a nice person. If she weren't dating my dad, and if she weren't Tiara Girl's aunt, I think I'd like her. A little voice in my head asks if she deserves to get dumped with a fake letter.

But I squash all that stuff down: we've got a job to do!

"Okay," I say, taking charge. As soon as I say this, I finally feel like my old self. "We'll meet at Jerzey Mae's house tomorrow afternoon." My life is finally back on track. I take an enormous bite of pizza and swallow it, hoping I can keep the voice in my head quiet for just a little while longer.

Wednesday after school, Dad drops me off at the triplets' house. They live in a fancy house in a part of Harlem called Strivers' Row. Their dad lets me in. He's a college professor and always looks like he's working out some math problem in his head, even though he teaches African Studies.

He stares at me for a moment. I wait for him to stop thinking and realize that I'm standing there, which he eventually does. "Oh, hello, Terrel," he says. "Go on up—the girls are in Jerzey Mae's room." He drifts back into his study as I clomp up the thickly carpeted stairs.

I could have guessed that everyone would be in Jerzey Mae's room. JoAnn's room is strewn with clothes and sports equipment, so you can barely walk across the floor without tripping. It's no wonder she ended up with a cast on her leg. Jessica's room is tidy, but it's full of animals, like Shakespeare the rat and Edgar the mynah bird. Meeting in there is like trying to meet in the middle of a zoo.

Jerzey's room is as tidy and pink as Jerzey Mae's clothes. JoAnn and Al are sprawled on the floor, and Jessica and Brenda are sitting on the pink canopied bed. Epatha is digging through Jerzey Mae's closet, accidentally knocking things off hangers as she goes through the clothes. Jerzey Mae looks restless, as if it were taking every last ounce of restraint she had not to jump up and stop her.

Epatha holds up a pink sweater and cocks her eyebrow at it. "Girlfriend, you gotta get off this pink kick," she says. "Pink is nice, *claro*, of course. But why not try purple? Or green? Or blue? Or all three, like me?" She twirls around like a fashion model and strikes a dramatic pose.

"I like pink," Jerzey Mae says.

Epatha throws her hands up in the air. "I give up. Hey, T.!" she says, noticing me. "Ready for Operation Dump Marjory?"

"You bet I am," I say.

We get to work. With seven of us, there is a lot of arguing about what should go into the letter.

"Start off with *My dearest Marjory*," says Epatha. "That's how Papa starts his letters to *mi madre.* I snuck a peek at one once before Mama grabbed it away."

"Why does your dad call your mom Marjory?" JoAnn asks. "Isn't her name Maria?"

Epatha hits her with one of Jerzey Mae's sweaters.

"Come on, guys," I say. "It's what we say next that's important."

"Just write, *I can't go out with you anymore,*" says JoAnn. "Get to the point. Why pussyfoot around?"

Jessica disagrees. "The letter's going to make her sad. We should at least say some nice stuff about her."

Brenda perks up. "She knew quite a bit about blood circulation," she says.

"I was thinking more like a compliment about her looks," Jessica says.

Jerzey Mae, who is taking dictation, puts down her pink pencil to think. "In romance books, the man is always telling the woman

that her eyes are limpid pools."

None of us knows what limpid pools are, but it sounds good, so we decide to put it in.

Epatha paces around the room. "Oh! Her shoes were *fabulosos*, too. I think they were Kenneth Cole."

Jerzey Mae scribbles furiously.

"You need to say she shouldn't try to get in touch with him," Al says. "If she calls up to ask why he sent the letter, this whole plan's going to fall apart."

"Good idea," I say.

"She'll see him at ballet when she's picking up Tiara Girl," Epatha says.

We fall silent. "Well, we'll just tell her to ignore him," I say.

"Because talking to her would be too painful!" Epatha says triumphantly. "It would be a reminder of their ill-fated love."

". . . Ill . . . fated. . . . love . . ." Jerzey murmurs as she writes.

"How should we end it?" I ask. "It should be businesslike. It can't be too mushy, because he's breaking up with her."

Jessica jumps up. "I just saw a letter on Dad's desk. He's sending it to his publisher. That should be businesslike enough." She runs down to the study and returns with a sheet of paper, which she gives to Jerzey Mae to copy.

After a long discussion, we finally have a draft that includes everyone's ideas. "Read it back to us, Jerzey Mae," I say.

Jerzey Mae picks up the letter, clears her throat, and recites what she's written.

My dearest Marjory,

Your eyes are limpid pools, and you know a lot about the way the human heart and blood vessels function. Also, your

Kenneth Cole shoes are very nice.

I can't go out with you anymore. Please do not call me. Also do not talk to me at ballet, because it would be a painful reminder of our ill-fated love.

Thank you for your time and consideration.

Best regards,
Mr. Liu

"He's not going to sign a letter to his girl-friend 'Mr. Liu,' you goofball!" says JoAnn.

Jerzey Mae glares at her.

"His name's Bruce," I say quickly. "That's really good, Jerzey Mae."

Jerzey Mae says she'll print out the letter on her good stationery that night. I pull an envelope with Marjory's address written on it out of my backpack. "It's already stamped," I say. "So you can just stick it in a mailbox when you're done."

"How did you find out where she lives?" asks Brenda with interest. "Did you follow her home or something?"

I shake my head. "I looked in Dad's address book when he was in the shower." I hand Jerzey Mae the envelope. She tucks it into her desk.

"Well," Epatha says, "that was a good afternoon's work."

"Thanks, you guys," I say. "This should do the trick."

Chapter 15

The next day, I think about the letter every once in a while. If Jerzey Mae mails it today, it should definitely get to Marjory's by tomorrow, making Friday the best day ever—Grocery Shopping Day and No More Marjory Day. Maybe Marjory will be so mad that she'll make Tiara Girl take ballet classes somewhere else, because then Marjory won't have to run into Dad. That would be amazing. I wonder if it's too much to hope for?

Time drags on Thursday night. We get our mail around three in the afternoon, so if Marjory gets hers about then, she'll probably have the letter in—I count on my fingers—twenty hours . . . nineteen hours and fifty-five minutes . . . nineteen hours and fifty minutes . . .

Finally I realize that my staring at the clock isn't going to make the time pass any faster, so I go into Cheng's room. He's building a model airplane. "Want to help?" he says.

I hold the plastic parts together as he carefully applies glue. I like hanging out with Cheng. Even though he's my brother, he doesn't pick on me or talk down to me. I think I enjoy times like this the best: when we're working on something together and not even talking.

I hear something. It sounds like music. Cheng looks up from his desk and smiles.

"Hear that?" he asks.

I nod. "What is it?"

"Dad. Who do you think?" He focuses on the plane again and applies another layer of glue. "He's started singing again. Haven't you noticed?"

I hadn't. I guess I never paid attention. "I don't remember him ever singing," I say.

Cheng points his desk light at the plane so he can see it better. "You don't?" He delicately brushes glue onto a tiny part, then gently puts it into place on the tip of the right wing. "He sang all the time when I was little. He was even in a community opera production."

"Really?" I say. It's hard to imagine my dad in an opera.

Cheng nods. "After Mom died, he stopped singing. I almost forgot that he sang at all, until I heard him a few days ago." He smiles. "I'm really glad he's dating Marjory. He seems a lot happier. Have you noticed?"

I feel prickly and uncomfortable. "Not really," I say. This is mostly true. I've been so wrapped up in wanting to get Marjory out of our lives that I haven't really noticed how Dad's been acting.

I think about the letter. "Maybe they'll

break up," I say casually. "You never can tell what might happen."

Cheng lets go of the piece, and watches to make sure it stays in place. "I hope not," he says. "Losing Mom was really hard on all of us, but especially on him. I think he's been really lonely since she passed away."

"Lonely?" I say. "How can he be lonely? He has six kids! What's wrong with us?"

Cheng's eyes are tender. "*Nothing's* wrong with us, T. You know Dad loves us a lot. Look how hard he works to take care of us. But sometimes family isn't enough. You have Dad and Danny and Tai and Edward and me and Waylon, but what would your life be like without your ballet friends?"

I think of Epatha, with her crazy clothes, always speaking three different languages; Brenda, talking backward and carrying around all those medical books; Al, who just moved here last summer but is already a good friend; Jerzey Mae, who's not quite as fussy about stuff as she used to be; JoAnn, with her baseball caps and roomful of sports stuff; Jessica, with her poetry and her animals. What *would* my life be like without them?

Lonely.

"Hey, where are you going?" Cheng asks.

I turn around at his door. "I gotta do something," I say.

I go back into my room and shut the door so I can't hear Dad singing. I feel low and mean. Suddenly I remember Tiara Girl's friend saying Marjory looked happy, and Tiara Girl replying, "I don't *care* if my aunt's happy!" in a really ugly voice.

I wanted Dad and Marjory to break up because I wanted things to be easier for me. I didn't think about Dad's feelings at all. I'm as bad as Tiara Girl. Actually, I'm worse. At least Tiara Girl didn't actually try to break Marjory and Dad up.

I have a great dad, and I've just ruined his life. I really am Terrible Terrel.

I run over to my backpack, dig out my phone, and dial. After a few rings, Jerzey Mae picks up.

"Did you mail that letter?" I ask. My heart is pounding. Maybe it's not too late.

"Don't worry," she says, sounding pleased with herself. "I put it in the mailbox on the way to school today. Marjory should definitely have the letter tomorrow."

"Oh, man," I say.

"What's wrong?" she asks.

"Nothing," I say. "I'll talk to you later, okay?"

Clearly there's only one thing to do. I've got to get that letter back before Marjory sees it.

Chapter 16

I run back into Cheng's room, where he's gluing a wing flap on a model airplane's left wing. "You have to help me," I say.

"With your homework? Sure," he says. "Just let me finish sticking this on."

"No!" I say. My voice sounds strained and a little bit panicky.

Cheng looks up at me in alarm. "What is it, T.? Are you okay?"

I shake my head. How much should I tell him? In the last ten minutes I've gone from thinking I'm a genius to thinking I'm the worst kid in the world. Cheng isn't mean and horrible like I am. I can't bring myself to tell him what I've done.

"Can you take me somewhere tomorrow after school?" I say.

"What's going on, Terrel?" Cheng asks.

"Please don't ask me any questions, okay?" I realize with alarm that I might start crying, and bite my lip hard to stop myself.

Cheng is clearly surprised to see me out of control like this. He closes his eyes tightly, as if he were wrestling with my request, but finally says, "Okay, T. No questions, as long as you promise me you're not going to do something stupid."

"I'm not," I say. "I'm trying to undo something stupid I already did."

He nods. "All right. I'll pick you up after school tomorrow, and we can go where you want. But I'm staying with you."

I take a deep breath. Now I just have to hope we can get to the letter before Marjory does.

* * *

Cheng is waiting for me outside after school the next day. It's clear but really cold. When I breathe in, my nostrils stick together. When I breathe out, a white cloud forms in front of my face. I pull up my jacket hood and stamp my feet; my toes are already turning into blocks of ice, and I've only been outside thirty seconds.

"Where are we going?" Cheng asks.

I show him the address. Luckily, Marjory lives only about fifteen blocks away. We walk quickly and don't talk. I wonder how we're going to get the letter back once we're there. Our mailbox is in the lobby of our building. You need a key to get inside the lobby, and you need a key to open the mailbox. I brought a bobby pin because I saw an old movie where someone used a bobby pin to pick a lock. But I'm thinking Cheng isn't going to keep his no-questions promise if I start breaking into a building.

Maybe we'll get there before the mail
carrier. "If you ask a mailman for a letter you
didn't mean to send, does he give it back to
you?" I ask.

"I don't think so, T.," Cheng says. "That's
tampering with the mail. It's against the
law."

Great. I wonder if they throw eight-year-olds in jail. A feeling of desperation crawls up from my stomach into my throat.

The one good thing is that it's early, so Marjory's probably still at work. I just have to hope that she has one of those mail slots in her door. If she does, maybe I can stick my hand in and fish the letter out.

Finally we turn onto Marjory's street. I check the numbers as we go.

"There it is," Cheng says. "Number forty-seven."

Marjory's house is one of those old brown-stones. And I'm relieved to see that there *is* a mail slot in the door. It even looks pretty wide; I'll bet my hand will fit. And, best of all, I see a mail carrier at the end of the next block. She must have delivered Marjory's mail just a few minutes ago.

I'm flooded with happiness. Just one more minute and this will all be over. I won't be

Terrible Terrel anymore; I'll just be a normal kid whose dad is dating some lady. It could be a lot worse.

I run up the steps, kneel down, and push up my jacket sleeve so I can stick my hand in the mail slot.

That's when the door opens.

It's Marjory.

Chapter 17

During our science lesson at school, we talked about prey animals. Those are the animals that other animals hunt. Instead of running away from danger, some prey animals freeze, in hopes that the hunter animal won't notice them. That seemed really stupid to me until just this very moment. Because when Marjory says hello, I automatically freeze. I don't even breathe. I just crouch down there by her door, as if somehow she won't see me, even though I'm wearing a bright orange coat and a pink scarf.

"Hello, Terrel," she says. "Are you looking for this, by any chance?"

She holds out a letter. I recognize Jerzey's

small, neat handwriting.

The letter is on pink stationery.

Pink! How could Jerzey Mae have used pink stationery? Of course Marjory must have known it wasn't from my dad. I didn't have to drag Cheng down here or anything. I didn't "save" Dad's relationship after all. Instead, I just got myself into trouble.

I slowly stand up.

"Would you like to come in?" she asks. "Is that one of your brothers out there?"

Cheng is hiding behind a tree, but his coat's kind of puffy, so it sticks out. He slowly appears.

"You come in, too," she says.

We walk into Marjory's house. It feels warm and homey. The walls are painted a buttery yellow, and a carpet blanketed with yellow roses covers the living room floor. It's not a fancy house, just a nice one.

"I think you and I should have a little

talk," she says to me. "Cheng, why don't you hang out in my office? I've got a few games on my computer if you're interested. It's the room all the way down on the right." She points down the hall.

He looks at me with concern, reluctant to leave me, but what choice does he have? He heads toward her office.

Marjory turns to me. "Want something to drink?"

I shake my head. She doesn't look mad, but some people don't look mad even when they are. They just look normal until they start screaming or throwing things at you. I'm really hoping Marjory isn't one of those people.

"Sit down, Terrel," she says, motioning to the couch. I sit down and sink back into the cushions, which are soft and comfortable.

"You look like you're freezing," says Marjory, which I am. She takes an orange blanket from the back of the couch and drapes it over me, then sits in a yellow armchair beside the couch.

"So. Want to tell me about that letter?" she asks. Her voice is gentle.

I say the first thing that pops into my head. "Not really."

She chuckles. "Maybe I should try that again. Why did you write the letter? I assume it *was* you who wrote it."

I suppose I could get off on a technicality here and say I didn't, since Jerzey Mae actually did the writing. But I say, "Yeah, I wrote it." I shift on the couch. "Are you going to tell my dad?"

She seems to be evaluating this. "I might not need to do that," she says. "Maybe we can keep it just between us girls."

I slowly let out the big breath I hadn't realized I'd been holding.

She continues. "But we do need to talk

about this, Terrel. Are you unhappy that your dad and I are going out?"

I don't know how to answer this. I'm not as unhappy as I was a few days ago. Now I get it that Dad needs a friend who's not one of us kids. But the idea of some woman coming in and taking over the grocery shopping and maybe even taking over my household binder still makes me feel mad and helpless.

"Your dad and I haven't been dating very long, but we've gotten to know each other pretty well outside your ballet classes over the last year or so. He's a wonderful man, and I know how much he loves you kids," she says.

There's a vase of flowers on a shelf right in front of me. I look at them so I don't have to look at Marjory.

She continues. "He's told me how much you do to keep the family running smoothly. The shopping, and reminding your brothers about their homework, and organizing everything. I think he wishes you didn't have to take on so much responsibility. That you had more time just to be a kid. Maybe if he and I keep seeing each other, I can help with—"

"No!" I say, in a louder voice than I'd intended. I sit straight up on the couch, as if it had been trying to swallow me up and I'd just realized it and managed to get away. "I like doing all that stuff. It's my *job*. If I don't do it, I'm not important. If I don't do it, no one will need me."

She sits silently, digesting what I've said. After a minute, she comes over and sits beside me on the couch. She looks at me, her eyes soft. "Terrel, you're important no matter what you do. Doing those things is a huge help to your dad, but you're important just because you're Terrel. Do you understand?"

I feel my eyes start to water. I pretend I have an itch so I can brush the tears away.

Marjory puts her arm around me lightly. "And can I tell you a secret?"

I'm silent because I don't want my voice to crack.

She goes on. "I am a *terrible* organizer. If your dad and I end up together—and that's a big if, because as you know, we are just getting to know each other—I would be thrilled if you kept on directing the grocery-shopping trips. And organizing your brothers. And frankly, I could use some help right away with this Nutcracker School holiday party next week. April volunteered me to be in charge of it. I don't even know where to start, so I keep putting it off. You think you might have room in your organizing schedule for one more disorganized person?"

Suddenly I feel much lighter, as if I'd been carrying a backpack full of Danny's body-building weights but it had suddenly disappeared. I nod.

Marjory smiles. "Good. Now. Is there anything else that's bothering you?"

I close my eyes to think, and a tiara flashes into my mind. I'm so happy about the organizing stuff that I hate to bring it up. But I guess we might as well get everything over with at once.

The words rush out of my mouth. "If you and Dad did . . ."—I can't quite bring myself to say *get married*—"If you did end up together, would I have to hang out with Tiara Girl all the time?" Panic shoots through my body as I realize my faux pas. "I mean, uh, with April?"

Marjory just looks at me. I can't tell if she's mad or not. "You call April 'Tiara Girl'?" she asks.

I can hardly deny it now. "Yeah."

Suddenly, she starts laughing, a rich, full, hearty laugh. "No wonder you looked so miserable in that tiara I gave you!" she says.

"Oh, honey, I had no idea. I'm sorry. I thought you'd like it." She laughs long and hard, and I can't help smiling.

"It is very, uh, sparkly," I say, trying to be nice.

Marjory wipes her eyes and turns to face me again. "Terrel, April is my niece, and I love her. But I understand that sometimes she's not the easiest kid to be around. Her parents are getting a divorce, and she's having a tough time."

This is a weird thought. It never occurred to me that Tiara Girl might be a jerk because she's unhappy.

Marjory goes on, "That's one of the reasons I take her on Saturdays. So, no, I would not expect you to be her best friend. But you might have to spend some time with her. Do you think you could do that, for your dad's sake?"

Between my friends and me, we've put a

spider into Marjory's drink, attacked her nose with a stink bomb, blasted her eardrums with horrible music, snuck a human heart into her briefcase, and written a letter that could have ruined her relationship (if Jerzey Mae hadn't written it on pink paper). I guess if she's not mad about any of that, I can put up with Tiara Girl . . . I mean, April.

"Okay," I say.

Marjory grins at me. "Can I have a hug?"

I hug her. Her sweater feels soft and cuddly, like my favorite teddy bear when I was a kid.

Marjory stands up. "Now. You and Cheng had better get on home," she says. She pokes her nose out the front door. "*Brrr*—it's getting even colder out there. You need any more clothes? A sweater or a hat?"

I shake my head.

She grins mischievously. "How about a nice, cozy tiara?"

Chapter 18

It's party time, and the Nutcracker School looks great. We took over one of the dance studios for our holiday party, and Marjory, Dad, and all my friends helped decorate (I organized, of course). Colorful streamers are draped across the ceiling. There's a Christmas tree, a Hanukkah menorah, and Kwanzaa candles. We turned off the main studio lights so the little red, blue, green, and yellow lights we strung around the room would shine more brightly.

The studio is full of ballet kids in party clothes and the kids' parents, all having a good time. Epatha's mom and dad made food for the party. Some local businesses donated prizes for a raffle. (My idea. I *am* good, if I do say so myself.) JoAnn volunteered to take care of the music, and holiday songs are blasting through the sound system. Ms. Debbé has already told her three times to turn it down.

We look outside the big studio windows; snowflakes are gently drifting down. It's a perfect way to end our fall ballet term.

"Want some?" Epatha offers me a cup of red punch with an orange slice floating in it. I take a sip. There must be soda in it, because it fizzes and tickles my nose.

"Thanks," I say.

My friends and I are gathered together by the window. Jerzey Mae is actually wearing red instead of pink, in honor of the season. We stand together quietly and watch our parents. Al's mom twirls to show off the puffy silver cone she is wearing for a hat, in combination with a silver dress, to the triplets' mom. Epatha's mom and dad look like they're sharing a joke as they serve food. Brenda's mom and the triplets' dad are chatting in the corner.

My dad and Marjory are standing together. Dad looks up and sees that they're right under the mistletoe hanging from the center of the ceiling. He leans forward and gently kisses Marjory on the lips. Not a big, gross kiss; just a little one.

I try to decide what I think about this.

I guess it's okay.

Tiara Girl is standing on the other side of the room with her friend. She must have seen the

kiss, too. She catches my eye. We look at each other for a long minute. Then she raises an eyebrow, shrugs her shoulders in a what-can-you-do? gesture, and turns back to her friend.

I feel an arm around me. "You okay, T.?" Al asks.

I nod. "Yup," I reply.

The music changes from a Christmas carol to a hip-hop song. "Who wants to dance?" I ask.

I start, my friends join in, and we dance until we can't dance anymore.

Terrel's Guide to Ballet Terms

châiné turns—quick turns that move across the room. I do these faster than a certain classmate, probably because the weight of the tiara on her head slows her down.

chassé—a move kind of like a gallop, where you jump through the air and one leg follows the other one. Chassés get you from one place to another quickly. This could be helpful if you're trying to run away from a stink bomb.

dating—when you go out with another person and maybe fall in love with them. Dating doesn't have much to do with ballet, unless your dad starts talking to another kid's aunt while they're waiting for your dance class to finish.

grocery shopping—going to the store and ordering your brothers around so your food gets bought in a very organized manner. Then you eat the food, which gives you energy to do ballet. Grocery shopping is NOT a good activity for a first date.

jeté—leap. When you find a human heart beside your briefcase, you might jeté across the room in fear. Unless you're Marjory, in which case you just talk about ventricles and stuff.

plié—knee bend. When you go all the way down, it's called a grand plié. Pliés make your legs strong, in case you need to jump up to get the peanut butter that your dad's girlfriend put away in the wrong cupboard.

tendu—when you stretch your foot out to the front, back, or side, but your foot doesn't leave the floor. If you tendu at exactly the right wrong time, someone walking by might trip over your foot and her tiara might fall off.

tiara—a sparkly crownlike thing you wear on your head if: (A) you are a princess, (B) you are an annoying kid in a ballet class, or (C) your dad makes you.